# My Secret Unicorn

## The Magic Spell

Lauren tried to imagine her pony. What colour would he be? How old? Maybe he would be a black pony with four white socks, or a flashy chestnut or a snow-white pony with a flowing mane and tail. Lauren smiled to herself. Yes, that's what she'd like – a beautiful white pony.

*Books in the series*

# My Secret Unicorn

## The Magic Spell

# Linda Chapman

*Illustrated by Biz Hull*

PUFFIN

PUFFIN BOOKS

UK | USA | Canada | Ireland | Australia
India | New Zealand | South Africa

Puffin Books is part of the Penguin Random House group of companies
whose addresses can be found at global.penguinrandomhouse.com.

www.penguin.co.uk    www.puffin.co.uk    www.ladybird.co.uk

First published 2002
This edition published 2018

005

Written by Linda Chapman
Text copyright © Working Partners Ltd, 2002
Illustrations copyright © Biz Hull, 2002
Created by Working Partners Ltd, London W6 0QT

The moral right of the author and illustrator has been asserted

Typeset in 14.25/21.5 pt Bembo
Printed in Great Britain by Clays Ltd, Elcograf S.p.A.

A CIP catalogue record for this book is available from the British Library

ISBN: 978-0-241-36916-6

All correspondence to:
Puffin Books
Penguin Random House Children's
80 Strand, London WC2R 0RL

*To Peter, for believing in dragons –*
*and in unicorns*

# Prologue

Deep in the mountains, mist swirled over a round stone table. A unicorn was standing beside it. With a snort, it lowered its noble head and touched the table's surface with its golden horn.

The table seemed to shiver for a moment. And then its surface began to shine like a mirror.

The unicorn murmured a name.

There was a flash of purple light and the mist cleared.

In the mirror, an image appeared. It was of a small grey pony.

Another unicorn came up to the table. It gazed at the grey pony thoughtfully. 'So, he is still looking for the right owner, to free his powers?' it said.

The golden-horned unicorn nodded its head. 'His last owner was often unkind.'

The other unicorn tossed its mane. Its silvery horn flashed in the light cast by the mirror. 'Surely, somewhere out there there must be someone who is good-hearted enough? Someone who has the imagination to believe in magic?'

'I think there is,' the golden-horned unicorn said softly. 'Watch. She is coming.'

★
★ ★

CHAPTER

# One

'Where do you want this box,
Mum?' Lauren Foster asked,
staggering into the kitchen.

Her mum was kneeling on the floor,
surrounded by packing cases. 'Just put it
anywhere you can find a space, honey,'
she said.

Lauren went over to the kitchen table
and put the box on it. Just then, Max, her

younger brother, came running in. Hot on his heels was Buddy, their ten-week-old Bernese mountain dog.

The puppy came bounding across the floor to say hello – and crashed straight into a stack of crockery that Mrs Foster had just unpacked. A couple of plates fell off the pile with a horrible clatter.

'Oh, Buddy . . .' Mrs Foster sighed.

'It's not his fault,' Max said. He rushed over to scoop the fluffy black and tan puppy into his arms. 'He just hasn't got the hang of stopping yet.'

Mrs Foster laughed. 'Why don't you take Buddy out into the yard?' she suggested. 'You can teach him how to use his brakes.'

Max and Buddy rushed out again into the April afternoon sunshine.

'Watch out, Max!' Mr Foster called from the hallway.

Lauren looked over and saw that Max and Buddy had almost tripped up two removal men on their way out.

Mr Foster, Lauren's dad, was directing the men, who were carrying furniture in from the removal lorry.

'What shall I do now, Dad?' Lauren asked.

'Coming through!' another removal man shouted, drowning out her dad's reply.

Lauren dodged out of the way as the man marched past, carrying the family computer. Mr Foster pushed a hand through his curly brown hair. 'Perhaps it would be best if you went and unpacked your bedroom, honey?' Without giving her a chance to reply, he hurried after the man with the computer. 'Please be careful! That's a delicate piece of equipment!'

Lauren grinned. It was a good idea to escape to her room!

It was strange to think that this house – Granger's Farm – was now her home. As she walked upstairs, Lauren thought about her two best friends back in the city, Carly and Anna. What would they be doing now? Maybe they'd be playing horses or eating the home-made pizzas that Anna's mum often made. Lauren wondered if they were missing her.

Feeling a little lonely, she walked along the landing to the bedroom at the far end and pushed open the white-painted wooden door. Her new room was small with a sloping ceiling. Sunlight streamed into the room through a little window.

Lauren stepped over the piles of boxes and suitcases and sat down on the window-seat to gaze at the view. The towering Blue Ridge Mountains in the distance were majestic and beautiful, but her eyes passed over them and fell on something much nearer to home: the little paddock and stable behind the house.

As she looked at them, her loneliness lifted. She might not know anyone here

in the country but at least she was going
to get a pony! A chance to have their own
animals had been the first thing her
parents had promised when they'd told
her and Max about moving from the city.

Mr Foster had decided to follow his dream of becoming a farmer. Max had chosen to have a puppy. They'd got Buddy a couple of weeks ago, and he was already a big part of the family. Everyone loved him. But for as long as Lauren could remember, she had wanted a pony of her own. And her mum was taking her to a horse and pony sale the very next day!

Lauren tried to imagine her pony. What colour would he be? How big? How old? Maybe he would be a black pony with four white socks, or a flashy chestnut or a snow-white pony with a flowing mane and tail. Lauren smiled to herself. Yes, that's what she'd like – a beautiful white pony.

'Lauren!'

Lauren's eyes shot open. It was her mum, calling from the landing. Lauren went to the door.

'I've unpacked some cookies,' her mum said. 'Why don't you come and have some with Max?'

'OK,' Lauren replied. And she went back down to join her family.

By the time Lauren went to bed that night, her bedroom was beginning to look more as if it belonged to her. Her clothes were hanging up in the closet and she had unpacked her books and cuddly toys.

Mrs Foster gently smoothed Lauren's hair. 'Time to get some sleep.'

Suddenly, Lauren didn't want to be left

alone. This was the first night in their new home and it felt a bit strange. 'Will you read me a story, Mum?' she asked. Now that she was nine she didn't usually have a bedtime story. But this was an unusual night.

Her mum seemed to understand. 'Of course, honey,' she said. 'Which one do you want?' She looked at the bookshelf.

'*The Little Pony*,' Lauren said, snuggling down beneath the duvet. *The Little Pony* was her favourite story. Mrs Foster was a writer and she'd written the story especially for Lauren when Lauren was just three years old. It was about a little white pony who travelled the world trying to find a home. He had almost given up when, one day, he met a girl who became his friend. And from then on, they'd looked after each other.

Her mum sat down on the bed and opened the book. As always, she started at the very first page. 'To Lauren, my very own little girl,' she read out softly. And then she started the story. 'Once upon a time, there was a little white pony who wanted a home . . .'

Lauren shut her eyes and smiled at the familiar, comforting words of the story. Halfway between wakefulness and sleep, plans for the next day went round in her head. They were going to a horse and pony sale! *This time tomorrow*, she thought, *I'll have a pony of my own.*

# CHAPTER
# Two

Soon after breakfast, Lauren set off
with her mother for the sale. They left
Max and her father at home with Buddy.

Even though it was raining, the
parking area was already very busy when
they arrived. Horses were being led
about and the air was filled with shouts
and whinnies. Loose dogs darted in
between people's legs. Stable-hands

dashed around with grooming brushes and saddles.

Lauren felt very excited. 'Where do we go?' she asked.

Her mum pointed out a sign that said LIVESTOCK. 'The horses and ponies will be over there. The bidding should have just started.'

Lauren followed her mum through the crowds until they came to a large covered ring.

A bay horse was being trotted around the ring by a stable-hand. A man standing on a platform at one end was calling out a price, raising his voice above the noise of the rain drumming on the roof. 'One thousand, two hundred dollars I'm bid.

Do I have any advance on one thousand, two hundred?'

A woman near Lauren held up her hand.

The man nodded at her. 'One thousand, three hundred to the lady on my left. Any advance on one thousand, three hundred dollars?'

Lauren turned to her mum. 'So the person who offers the most money gets the horse?'

Her mum nodded. 'The auctioneer – that's the man on the platform – keeps raising the price until no one else bids.'

'Any advance on one thousand, three hundred?' the auctioneer shouted. No one moved. He raised a small wooden hammer. 'Going, going – gone!' he said, bringing the hammer down on the table beside him with a bang. 'Sold to the lady on my left.'

The lady smiled and the horse was led out of the ring. A new horse – a big dapple-grey – was brought in by another stable-hand.

'Come on, let's go and look around,' Mrs Foster said to Lauren. She led the way towards an enormous barn beside the ring. Lauren gasped when she looked inside. It was full of pens and nearly all had horses standing in them. There were bays and chestnuts and greys, each awaiting their turn in the ring. Lauren thought they all looked very big.

Lauren's mother had disappeared ahead

of her through a gate, but Lauren didn't want to walk too quickly; she didn't want to miss a thing. Carefully she picked her way through the puddles underfoot and made her way through the crowd. She reached the gate at the same time as an elderly lady who was sheltering beneath a brightly coloured umbrella. Lauren held the gate open for her.

The lady nodded. 'Thank you,' she said.

Lauren followed her through. The lady suddenly slipped on the wet ground and almost fell. 'Careful!' Lauren cried. She reached forward to hold the lady's elbow until she had regained her balance.

'Thank you again,' the lady said, her face creasing into a wide smile. She had

the friendliest blue eyes that Lauren had
ever seen.

'You're welcome,' Lauren said, smiling.
'I'm Lauren,' she went on.

'Hello, Lauren,' the lady answered. 'So
if you're here at the sale, I guess you like
ponies.'

Lauren nodded. 'I love them! My parents are going to buy me one.' She didn't want to sound spoilt, but she couldn't stop herself from blurting out her amazing news.

'Aren't you lucky?' The lady's eyes twinkled as they met Lauren's.

'I'm the luckiest person in the world,' Lauren breathed. 'Will you be OK now? I ought to get going. My mother will be wondering where I am.'

'I'll be just fine, thank you,' the lady replied. 'I hope you find the pony you're looking for.'

'Thank you,' Lauren said. She scanned the crowds anxiously for her mother. Spotting her, she looked back to say goodbye to the old lady, but she had already slipped away.

Lauren shrugged and quickly made her way into the barn, past the horses. As she rounded the corner, she saw her mum ahead of her, at the end of the barn. She was standing beside a row of about ten ponies. Lauren ran to her.

'There you are, Lauren!' her mother exclaimed. 'I thought I'd lost you.'

'Not a chance,' Lauren grinned. She looked excitedly at the ponies in front of her.

In the first pen, there was a tiny black pony. The next pen was empty, but beside it there were two pretty chestnuts with matching white stars. Next to them was an old grey mare with feathery legs and a large head, and beside her was a cheeky-looking bay. On the door of each pen there was a card with details about the pony inside.

There was no sparkling white pony like Lauren had been imagining, but she didn't care. 'They're all lovely!' she gasped, turning around to her mum.

'Well, this one's much too small,' Mrs Foster said, as she looked at the little black pony. 'We want a pony who's about thirteen hands high and at least six years old. Any younger and he'll be too inexperienced.'

Lauren ran over to the bay gelding's pen and looked at the card attached to his gate. 'Topper,' she read out. 'Thirteen hands. Four years old.' She felt a flicker of disappointment. He was too young. She patted him and moved on.

The grey mare was too tall, the black pony was too small, and the chestnut ponies were only three years old. Lauren walked along the line of ponies, reading their sale notices. She reached the end of the row. Not one of them was right.

Her mum came up behind her and squeezed her shoulder. 'Maybe we won't find your perfect pony today. We can always come to the next sale. It's only a month away.'

*A month!* Lauren looked around. She couldn't wait that long. 'The little black pony isn't that small,' she began desperately. 'And he's really cute . . .'

Just then, she heard the sound of hooves. She swung around. A man was leading a scruffy grey pony out of the vet's tent and down the walkway towards the last empty pen. 'I thought I wasn't going to get here in time for the sale,' he said, noticing Lauren and her mum.

The pony looked quiet and sad.

'Hi, boy,' Lauren said, going over to him.

At the sound of her voice, the pony lifted his head and pricked his ears. He whinnied and Lauren felt her heart flip. Suddenly she didn't care that he was scruffy and dirty. This was the pony she wanted. 'How old is he?' she asked the pony's owner.

'Twilight? He's seven,' the man replied.

Lauren swung around to her mum. 'He's the right age!' The pony stepped forward and thrust his nose into her hands. His breath was warm as he nuzzled at her fingers.

'Can we buy him?' Lauren asked her mother eagerly.

The man smiled at them. 'Are you looking for a pony?'

'Yes, we are,' Mrs Foster replied. She walked forward and looked at Twilight. 'Why's he for sale, Mr –?'

'Roberts – Cliff Roberts,' the man said, introducing himself and shaking hands.

'The pony's for sale because my daughter, Jade, doesn't want him any more,' he explained. 'I only bought Twilight for her a few months ago but she says he's too quiet and not showy enough. I've just bought her a new pony to take to shows, so now I've got to sell Twilight.'

'Can we buy him?' Lauren asked her mum again.

'Well, you'll have to have a ride on him first,' her mum said. She turned to Twilight's owner. 'Would that be possible, Mr Roberts?'

Mr Roberts smiled. 'Of course. It looks like the rain has stopped now. I'll just go and get the saddle.'

★

Five minutes later, Lauren found herself
riding Twilight around the exercise
paddock. He felt wonderful. The slightest
squeeze of her legs made him go faster
and the smallest pull on the reins slowed
him down. It was almost as though he
could read her mind.

'That's amazing!' Mr Roberts said, as
Lauren brought Twilight to a halt by the
paddock gate and dismounted. 'He hardly
wanted to do anything for Jade. He must
like you.'

'I love him!' Lauren said, her eyes
shining. She stretched out her hands
towards Twilight. The pony lowered his
muzzle and blew softly on Lauren's face.
'Please can we buy him?' she begged her

mother. 'He's perfect!'

'He certainly seems very well behaved,' Mrs Foster said, patting Twilight. 'Maybe we'll bid for him when he goes into the ring.'

Lauren thought about the sale and the way the person who offered the most money got the pony. 'But someone else might bid more than us,' she said in alarm. 'Can't we just buy him now?'

'I'm quite happy to arrange a private sale, if you're interested,' Mr Roberts said to Lauren's mother. 'I wouldn't have to pay the auction fee then, so it would save me some money. How about we say . . .' He thought for a moment and then named a price. 'I'll even throw in the saddle and bridle if you like.'

Lauren looked at her mum and crossed her fingers. She didn't think she could bear to see Twilight go into the ring and be sold to someone else. *Oh, please*, she prayed. *Please say yes*.

To her amazement, her mum smiled. 'OK, Mr Roberts. You've got yourself a deal.'

Lauren could hardly believe it. She threw her arms round Twilight's neck and hugged him. 'Oh, Twilight!' she gasped in delight. 'You're going to be mine!'

The little grey pony nuzzled her happily, as if he understood.

CHAPTER

# Three

It was soon arranged that Mr Roberts
would drive Twilight round to
Granger's Farm the next morning.

'That gives us time to buy everything
we need and get the paddock and stable
ready,' Mrs Foster said to Lauren.

On the way home Lauren and her
mum drove to the local tack store on the
outskirts of the town.

The sales assistant, a girl called Jenny,
was very helpful. Soon there were loads
of horsy things on the counter – brushes,
a first-aid kit, feed buckets, a head-collar.
The pile grew bigger and bigger until, at
last, Lauren had everything she needed.

Jenny helped them pack all their
purchases into their car. 'Have fun with
your new pony!' she called to Lauren.

Lauren grinned at her. 'Thanks! I will!'

As Jenny went back to the store, Lauren
noticed a small bookshop tucked
between the tack store and a shop selling
electrical goods. It had an old-fashioned
brown and gold sign over the window
saying MRS FONTANA'S NEW
AND USED BOOKS. 'Look at that

bookshop, Mum,' she said.

'Shall we take a look inside?' Mrs
Foster asked.

Lauren nodded eagerly. Both she and
her mum loved bookshops, and this one
looked really interesting.

They walked along the pavement.
Through the glass panel in the door,
Lauren could see a cheerful rose-
patterned carpet, and shelves and shelves
of books.

Mrs Foster pushed the door open. A
bell tinkled and they stepped inside.

'Wow!' Lauren said, looking around.
There were books everywhere! Old
books, new books – and not just on the
shelves. There were piles of books next to

the shelves. And more piles in front of those! But enough space had been left for a few chairs to be placed round a pretty iron fireplace. A large notice said: *Please feel free to browse and sit awhile.* It was the strangest, loveliest bookshop that Lauren had ever been in.

Just then there was a pattering of feet, and a little white terrier dog with a black patch over one eye came trotting up to them. 'Look, Mum!' Lauren exclaimed. She crouched down and the terrier licked her hand.

Mrs Foster bent down to stroke him. 'Hi, little one,' she said.

'Isn't he cute?' said Lauren.

'Ah, I see you've met Walter.'

Lauren and her mum looked up. An elderly lady was coming towards them. She was wearing an embroidered shawl over a flowery dress. Lauren gasped. It was the lady she'd met at the horse sale earlier! There was no mistaking the warm blue eyes.

'Hello, Lauren,' the lady said, smiling.

'You two know each other?' Lauren's mother said, looking surprised.

'We met at the horse and pony sale this morning,' the lady explained. She held out her hand. 'I'm Mrs Fontana,' she said. 'This is my shop.'

'Alice Foster,' Lauren's mum said, shaking hands. 'We've just moved into the area. Is it OK if we have a look around?'

'Feel free,' Mrs Fontana replied. She smiled at Lauren. 'There are lots of books in the side room you might like.'

Leaving her mum to browse, Lauren made her way to the side of the shop. The next room was full of children's books. There were no bright posters or colourful displays like there were in most bookshops, but there were lots of plump, soft cushions on the floor and a big table piled high with all kinds of books.

Lauren examined each pile and quickly picked out a collection of pony stories. She sat down on one of the cushions and started to read.

Suddenly she heard the patter of paws coming towards her. It was Walter, the

terrier. He sat down beside Lauren and looked at her, his head cocked on one side. Lauren tickled him under the chin.

'He likes you,' Mrs Fontana said.

Lauren jumped. The old lady seemed to

have appeared out of nowhere.

She smiled again at Lauren. 'So what have you chosen, my dear?'

Feeling slightly shy, Lauren showed Mrs Fontana the book of pony stories.

'I thought you might like those,' Mrs Fontana said, raising her bright eyes to Lauren's face. 'Did you find your pony today?'

'I certainly did,' Lauren said, nodding excitedly. 'He's coming tomorrow. He's called Twilight and he's wonderful!'

Mrs Fontana stared at her for a moment and then she swung around. 'You know what?' she said. 'I think I might have just the thing for you. It's up here.'

Lauren watched as Mrs Fontana fetched a folding stepladder and stood on it to reach the top shelf. 'Here we are,' the old lady said, pulling out a dusty purple book. She climbed down the ladder and handed the book to Lauren.

Lauren looked down at the heavy leather volume. It had beautiful gold writing on the cover. Lauren looked at the words. '*The Life of a Unicorn*,' she read out.

She opened the book. The pages were smooth and yellow with age. There was lots of writing, but also some beautiful pictures. Unicorns cantered in the sky and grazed on soft grass. 'They're lovely,' she said as she turned the pages.

'Yes,' Mrs Fontana agreed, sighing.

Lauren stopped at the next picture. There was no unicorn to be seen, just a small grey pony.

'That's a young unicorn,' Mrs Fontana said, looking over her shoulder.

'But it hasn't got a horn,' Lauren said.

'Ah, but, you see, young unicorns don't have horns,' Mrs Fontana told her. 'They only grow their horns and receive their magical powers when they hear some magic words on their second birthday. Then they turn into the creatures that we know as unicorns.'

Lauren looked at her in surprise. From the way Mrs Fontana was talking, she made it sound as if unicorns were real.

'But unicorns don't really exist, do they?' Lauren said to the old lady. 'They're just made up, like fairies and dragons and trolls.'

'You don't think fairies, dragons and trolls exist either?' Mrs Fontana said, raising her eyebrows.

'No way,' Lauren grinned.

'Why not?' Mrs Fontana said.

Looking into Mrs Fontana's blue eyes, Lauren suddenly felt less certain. 'Well, no one has ever seen them,' she faltered.

'Maybe that's because they don't *want* to be seen,' Mrs Fontana said. She looked around and then leaned forward. 'Shall I tell you a secret? I've seen a unicorn.'

Lauren stared at her in astonishment. Had Mrs Fontana gone crazy?

Mrs Fontana seemed to read her mind. 'Oh, I'm not mad, dear,' she said with a smile. 'All it needs are the magic words, spoken by the right person, a handful of the secret flowers – and a unicorn, of course.'

Just then there was the sound of footsteps. 'Are you ready, honey?' Mrs Foster asked. 'We should be going home.'

Mrs Fontana stood up briskly. Lauren felt as if she had been jerked out of a dream.

'What's that?' her mum said, seeing the book in Lauren's hands.

'A . . . a book on unicorns,' Lauren said, standing up.

Mrs Foster glanced at the book. She

took in the soft leather binding and the pictures, glowing in jewel colours. 'It looks very expensive, honey. I'm afraid we can't afford it,' she said.

Lauren nodded. She hadn't really expected her mum to buy it for her.

'I'd like you to have it,' Mrs Fontana said softly.

Lauren looked at her in amazement.

The old lady smiled. 'Think of it as a gift to welcome you to the town.'

'But, Mrs Fontana, that's much too generous . . .' Mrs Foster began.

'Not at all,' said Mrs Fontana. 'It's a very special book and it needs a good home. Something tells me that Lauren will look after it.'

'Oh, I will!' Lauren gasped. 'Thank you, Mrs Fontana.' She took the book in her hands and held it close to her.

The bookshop owner showed them to the door. 'Do call again,' she said. 'And good luck at Granger's Farm.'

'We will – and thank you so much for the welcome gift,' Mrs Foster said.

The door tinkled shut behind them. Lauren was suddenly struck by a thought. 'How did Mrs Fontana know that we had moved to Granger's Farm? We didn't tell her.'

Mrs Foster frowned. 'Didn't we?'

'No,' Lauren said.

Her mum shrugged. 'Oh, well, it's a small town. News has probably got around. Now, come on. Dad and Max will be wondering where we are.'

They got into the car. As her mum started the engine, Lauren looked back once more at the bookshop. Walter, the

little dog, was sitting in the window,
staring out. It looked just as if he was
smiling at them.

# Four

As Mrs Foster drove back to Granger's Farm, Lauren looked at the beautiful book she had been given. When she came to the page with the picture of the baby unicorn, she could almost hear Mrs Fontana's voice saying, *I've seen a unicorn.*

Lauren gently stroked the picture with her fingertip. She was sure that Mrs

Fontana must have been making up all that stuff about magical creatures. The old lady couldn't really have seen a unicorn.

Could she?

*Of course she couldn't,* Lauren told herself firmly. *Unicorns don't exist. Mrs Fontana has just been reading one too many of her old books.*

'So, what have you bought?' Mr Foster asked, coming out to meet them as they pulled up at the farm. Max ran out after him.

'Lots,' Lauren said, jumping out of the car.

'Can I see?' said Max, opening the back door. He pulled a hoof pick out of one of the bags. 'What's this for?'

'Come on, Max,' Mr Foster said. 'Lauren can explain while we unload.'

They carried the bags to the stable, and then Mrs Foster went into the house to do some more unpacking while Lauren, her dad and Max carried the purchases for Twilight into the little shed which was going to be his tack room. Mr Foster hammered two metal hooks into the wall, one for Twilight's bridle and one for his new red and blue head-collar. Then he fetched a low table and an old striped rug from the garage.

With the rug on the floor, a light bulb gleaming brightly and Lauren's shiny new grooming kit and first-aid box laid out

on the table, the tack room looked very
cosy and cheerful.

'This is great,' Lauren said, looking
around happily.

'Now all we need is Twilight,' Mr Foster said, smiling at Lauren.

Lauren imagined Twilight's grey head looking out over the stable door. 'I can't wait till tomorrow!' she said.

That night, when Lauren went to bed, she opened the book that Mrs Fontana had given her and began to read the first chapter. '*Noah and the unicorns*,' she whispered quietly to herself . . .

*Many years ago, there was a great flood that threatened both animals and magical creatures. The magical creatures fled to safety in Arcadia, an enchanted land that can't be found by humans.*

Meanwhile, a man called Noah gathered together two of every animal and took them on to the Ark he had built. As the rain started to fall, Noah saw two small grey ponies in the grassy meadows beside the rising sea. He took them on to his Ark with the rest of the animals.

Through a magic mirror, the unicorns in Arcadia watched gratefully as Noah took care of their young. For these two grey ponies were, in fact, baby unicorns who hadn't yet grown into their magical powers. They had been left behind in the rush to Arcadia.

Whilst on the Ark, the time for the two young unicorns to gain their magical powers came and went. They had lost their chance. And the unicorns in Arcadia mourned.

When a whole year had passed, the floods
went down. Noah released the young unicorns
on to the Earth with the other animals. And
there they remained, trapped in their pony
bodies.

Back in Arcadia, the watching unicorns
worked on a Turning Spell that would give the
unicorns another chance to gain their magical
powers. The spell took years and years to
perfect. At last it was ready. But the spell
would only free a unicorn if spoken by a good-
hearted human who believed in magic.

A very brave unicorn risked his own powers
to fly back to Earth. He searched long and
hard for a human to whom he could entrust
the spell. Eventually he found her.

The spell worked – and the two young

*unicorns became great friends with the human who had helped them. They grew beautiful horns and flew like angels. And together they had many magical adventures . . .*

CHAPTER

# Five

Lauren put the book down. The way the book was written made everything about unicorns sound so real, not like a made-up story at all. She looked at the picture at the end of the chapter. It showed a beautiful unicorn cantering up into the sky.

*I wish the story was true*, Lauren thought. *I wish there were still unicorns on the Earth.*

*I'd love to help one.*

And then she smiled. Unicorns might not exist, but Twilight did and he was going to arrive the very next day.

Mr Roberts arrived with Twilight at ten o'clock. He opened the side door of the trailer so that Lauren could get inside. Twilight whinnied as she stepped into the trailer.

'Hello, little one,' Lauren said, stroking his nose.

Twilight looked at her. *Hello*, his dark eyes seemed to say back.

Mr Roberts lowered the ramp to the ground. 'You can bring him out now, Lauren!' he called.

Lauren untied Twilight and backed carefully out of the trailer. Her mum and dad and Max came over.

'Hello, boy,' Mrs Foster said, feeding Twilight a carrot.

'He's really dirty, isn't he?' Max said, as he patted Twilight and a cloud of dust flew into the air.

Twilight whinnied indignantly, as if he understood what Max had said.

Mr Roberts smiled ruefully. 'I'm afraid my daughter has been busy with her new pony. She hasn't been looking after Twilight as well as she might.' He looked at Lauren. 'You'd like Jade. She's just crazy about ponies.'

Lauren wasn't so sure. If Mr Roberts's

daughter was really crazy about ponies, she would have looked after Twilight better. But she didn't say anything.

While Mr and Mrs Foster sorted out paying Mr Roberts, Lauren and Max led Twilight to his stable.

'Are you going to ride now, Lauren?' Max asked.

'I'm going to groom him first,' Lauren replied.

She tied Twilight up outside the stable and fetched the grooming kit.

'Can I help?' asked Max.

'OK,' Lauren said, handing him a brush with thick bristles called a dandy brush. It was good for getting rid of dirt and dust. 'You can brush him with that.'

Twilight nuzzled her shoulder. Lauren smiled happily and kissed his face. She didn't think she'd ever felt happier in her life.

Two hours later, Twilight was looking much smarter. Lauren and Max had brushed him and washed his mane and tail. Instead of being a dirty grey colour, he was now pale grey. The dust had come out of his coat and Lauren had replaced the old, tatty head-collar he had been wearing with the new red and blue one that she and her mum had bought the day before. However, despite everything, Twilight still looked a bit scruffy. His coat didn't really shine, and the long hair

around his hooves and under his chin was
quite straggly. Still, Lauren didn't mind.

With her mum's help, Lauren tacked

Twilight up and rode him into the paddock. Just like the day before, he seemed to know exactly what she wanted him to do, and soon they were cantering around the field. When Lauren finally stopped him by the gate, her face was flushed and her eyes were shining. 'He's just great!' she said to her mum, who was watching with Max. 'Can I go for a ride in the woods?' She saw her mum look doubtful. 'I won't go far.'

'OK,' Mrs Foster agreed. 'But don't stay out too long.'

'I won't. I promise,' Lauren said. She remounted and rode Twilight out of the paddock. The mountain that rose up behind the farmhouse was thickly wooded and, as she rode Twilight into the trees, she felt his ears prick and his step quicken.

Lauren smiled happily. 'You like it up here, don't you, boy?'

Twilight snorted and broke into a trot.

Lauren let him have his head and he broke into a canter. They made their way along the trail. The air was quiet so that the only sound, apart from the thudding of Twilight's hooves on the soft ground, was the distant calling of birds in the tops of the trees. Lauren felt that she could have gone on forever. But she remembered what she had promised her mum, so she slowed Twilight down to turn him around.

Twilight looked to one side. A small

side-trail led off the main track. He
pulled towards it. Lauren stopped him.
'No,' she told him. 'We've got to go back
now.' Twilight pulled towards the side-
trail again.

'We'll go another day,' Lauren told him and then, turning him around, she rode back to the farm.

That night, when Lauren went to bed, she opened the unicorn book to a beautiful picture showing unicorns grazing in lush meadows dotted with star-shaped purple flowers. The pink sky was streaked across with orange and gold, as if the sun was setting. She began to read . . .

*When the two young unicorns grew old they returned to Arcadia. The unicorn elders decided that from then on they would send young unicorns to Earth to do good works. They look like small ponies. Each of them hopes to find someone who will learn how to free their magical powers. To do this one needs: the words of the Turning Spell, a hair from the unicorn's mane, the petals from a single moonflower and the light of the Twilight Star, which only shines for ten minutes after the sun has set.*

Lauren turned the page and saw the picture of the young unicorn that she had seen in Mrs Fontana's shop. Scruffy and grey, it looked quite like Twilight.

*Maybe Twilight's a unicorn in disguise,* Lauren thought suddenly.

She smiled to herself. She was being silly. It was just a made-up story and Twilight was just a regular pony.

CHAPTER

# Six

After breakfast the next morning, Lauren took Twilight out for a ride in the woods again. It felt a bit lonely on her own. *I wish I had someone else to ride with*, she thought. She wondered if she would make friends with someone when school started.

As they reached the trees, Twilight pricked up his ears and pulled at the reins.

'OK, boy,' Lauren said, letting him trot.

She had been riding for ten minutes when Twilight suddenly stopped.

'Go on!' Lauren encouraged him.

But Twilight wouldn't move. He shook his head and looked to the left.

Lauren realized that he was looking along the same side-trail he had tried to go down the last time they had been in the woods. She thought for a moment. What harm could there be in exploring?

'All right,' she said, turning Twilight towards it.

The track was narrow and the trees on either side met over Lauren's head, blocking out the sun. It was like riding through a long, green tunnel. As the

silence closed in around them, Lauren
began to wonder where the track was
leading.

'Maybe we should turn back,' she
whispered to Twilight, but the pony
pulled eagerly on the reins. It was clear
he didn't want to stop.

Lauren saw light ahead. It looked as if
the track was coming to an end.
Wondering where they would come out,
she let Twilight carry on. He trotted out
from among the trees and into a grassy
glade.

It was beautiful. In the centre of the
glade there was a mound dotted with
purple flowers where a cloud of yellow
butterflies fluttered in the sunlight.

Twilight walked to the mound and
Lauren saw that the flowers were star-
shaped and at the tip of each bright petal

there was a golden spot. She frowned.
She knew she had seen them somewhere
before, but she couldn't remember where.

With a soft whicker, Twilight bent his head. Thinking he was grabbing a mouthful of grass, Lauren tried to pull his head up. 'No, Twilight!'

But as she spoke she realized that he wasn't eating, he was nuzzling at the star-shaped flowers. Her curiosity was aroused and she dismounted.

Looping the reins round her arm, she looked closely at the flowers. Where *had* she seen them before?

Twilight whickered and nudged her arm. Lauren was puzzled. It was as if he was trying to tell her something, she thought, then she shook her head.

*He's just a pony*, she reminded herself quickly.

She glanced around. The glade was so beautiful and still that she didn't want to leave. But she knew that she ought to be getting home, so she mounted Twilight and rode him back into the trees.

Lauren turned Twilight on to the main trail through the woods where the birds were singing overhead again. Leaning forward, she let him go faster and they cantered along the track towards home.

When they got back to the farm, Lauren went into the study, where her dad had loads of books about plants. She took the biggest one down from the shelf and began to look through the section on woodland flowers. There were quite a few plants with purple flowers but none of them was star-shaped with golden spots on the edge of the petals. She tried another book and then another. But she couldn't find any flowers that looked like the ones in the glade.

She closed the last book and sighed. She knew she had seen the flowers before somewhere.

'I thought I heard you in here,' Mrs Foster said, coming into the study. 'What are you doing?'

'I've been trying to find the name of some flowers I saw in the woods,' Lauren replied. She wondered if her mum would know what they were. 'They were purple, sort of star-shaped with a gold spot at the tip of each petal.'

'Sorry, I can't help you,' her mum said. 'They sound very unusual, though. Now,' she went on, changing the subject, 'we need to get you some things for school – you start next week. Why don't you run upstairs and get changed and we'll go to the mall?'

'OK,' Lauren said.

She hurried up to her room and pulled on a pair of clean jeans and a sweatshirt. The unicorn book was lying on her bedside table. It was still open at the picture of the unicorns grazing. As Lauren did up her jeans, she glanced at it again: the unicorns, the grassy meadows, the purple flowers . . .

*The purple flowers!*

She stared at the picture. They were exactly the same as the ones she had just seen in the wood!

CHAPTER

# Seven

Lauren snatched up the book. The flowers in the picture had the same star shape, the same gold spot. A wild thought filled her mind. The book had said that unicorns disguised as ponies could be changed back by saying a magic spell and using a certain type of flower. What if the flowers she had found in the wood were the very ones that were needed in the spell?

She quickly turned the pages of the book until she found the part that explained how unicorns disguised as ponies could be changed back into unicorns. In the middle of the page there was a small picture of a purple flower just like the ones in the wood. Lauren read the words under the picture.

*The moonflower: a rare purple-flowering herb that is used in the Turning Spell.*

Lauren stared. She'd found the flower that the book said could give a unicorn its magical powers. She remembered the way Twilight had been nuzzling at the flowers

in the glade. Maybe the story was true . . .
and maybe, just maybe, Twilight really was
a unicorn in disguise!

Her heart started to race. If she could

just find the words of the spell, then she could try it out.

'Lauren! Are you coming?' her mum called.

Lauren could hardly bear to put the book down. The spell had to be here somewhere.

'Lauren!' her mum called again.

Lauren closed the book reluctantly. 'I'm coming!' she called, and she went downstairs.

Normally Lauren loved buying things for a new school term, but not that day. All she could think about was unicorns.

On the way home, Mrs Foster stopped

by the tack store to pick up a couple of
spare feed buckets.

Lauren had an idea. 'Can I go and look
in the bookshop?' she asked.

'Sure,' Mrs Foster agreed. 'I'll meet you
there in a few minutes.'

Lauren ran to the bookshop. The
doorbell tinkled as she went inside. The
shop was just as she remembered it: the
piles of books, the rose-patterned carpet.
She caught sight of the owner near the
back of the shop. 'Mrs Fontana!' she
called.

The old lady turned around. 'Hello,
dear,' she said. 'What can I do for you?'

Suddenly Lauren didn't know what to
say. Mrs Fontana looked so calm and

ordinary that the whole idea of asking
her if she knew what the magic spell was
seemed really dumb. 'Um . . . well . . . I . . .'
Lauren stammered.

'So, have you seen a unicorn yet?' Mrs
Fontana said softly.

Lauren stopped stammering and stared.

'That's what you wanted to come in
and talk to me about, isn't it?' Mrs
Fontana said.

Lauren didn't even stop to ask how the
old lady knew. 'Is the story really true?'
she gasped.

Mrs Fontana smiled. 'It's true for those
who want it to be true.'

'Do you know what the spell is?'
Lauren asked eagerly.

'I do, but I can't tell you,' the old lady replied. 'Those who want to find unicorns must do it for themselves. You have everything you need.'

'But . . .' Lauren began.

Just then Walter gave a warning bark. The shop door swung open and Lauren's mum came in. 'Hello, Mrs Fontana,' she said.

'Hello,' the bookshop owner said with a smile. 'So how are you settling in at Granger's Farm?' Her tone changed and now she sounded brisk and efficient.

Lauren waited while the two adults chatted. She felt frustrated. If Mrs Fontana really knew what the spell was, why wouldn't she tell it to her? She longed to ask the bookshop owner more, but she couldn't with her mum standing there.

Lauren thought about the old lady's words: *You have everything you need*.

What did she mean?

That night, when she went to bed, Lauren decided to read the book from the beginning through to the end.

Starting at the first chapter, she began to read slowly and carefully. She read that after the floods had gone down, the magical creatures decided not to live on Earth any more and stayed in Arcadia. Arcadia was ruled by seven Golden Unicorns who watched the Earth through a magic mirror.

Lauren read on, but she didn't find the spell.

She awoke the following morning to see the book lying beside her on her bed. She had just two chapters left to read. She wondered whether to start on them, but then she saw that it was seven o'clock. It was time to get up and give Twilight his breakfast. She took the book outside with her. She could read it while he was eating.

Leaving it in the tack room, she brought Twilight in from the paddock and put him in his stall. Then she mixed up his feed. The sooner Twilight was fed, the sooner she could read a little more.

Quickly, Lauren emptied the feed into the manger and then she fetched the book. Carrying it into his stable, she sat down on an upturned bucket and began to read. Surely the spell had to be in the book somewhere!

Lauren became aware that Twilight had stopped eating. He was staring at the book. With a snort, he walked over to her.

'Hello, boy,' she said.

Twilight blew gently. The pages of the book fluttered over.

'Twilight! You've lost my place!' Lauren said. But before she could turn back to the page she had been reading, Twilight breathed out again.

'What are you doing?' Lauren asked, as
he nuzzled his soft lips against the back
cover. They left a damp mark on the

paper and she made to push his muzzle away but, as she did so, she realized that the last page of the book had been glued to the back cover. One corner of the page fluttered slightly as Twilight breathed on the book.

Lauren carefully pulled at it. The glue gave way and the page turned.

Inside the cover were some faint words written in pencil. It looked like a poem of some sort. Lauren read the title: *The Turning Spell*.

CHAPTER

# Eight

Trembling with excitement, Lauren
read the faintly pencilled words:

*Twilight Star, Twilight Star,*
*Twinkling high above so far.*
*Shining light, shining bright,*
*Will you grant my wish tonight?*
*Let my little horse forlorn*
*Be at last a unicorn!*

Her eyes flew to Twilight. 'Oh, Twilight,' she whispered. 'It's the spell!'

Twilight bent his head as if he was nodding.

Lauren jumped to her feet. She had to take Twilight to the woods and pick one of those flowers!

After giving Twilight time to digest his breakfast, Lauren tacked him up and rode into the woods. Twilight seemed to know just where they were going. With his ears pricked up he cantered along the track until they came to the little side-trail.

They turned down the narrow track and followed it until they reached the sunny glade. It looked just the same as the day before. A cloud of butterflies swooped over the grass and the air had an expectant feeling.

Lauren dismounted and led Twilight over to the grassy mound, where she found a single purple flower that had fallen to the ground. She picked it up. As she did so, a sharp tingle ran down her spine.

She felt Twilight's warm breath on her shoulder and she looked at him. 'Oh, Twilight,' she whispered. 'I hope this is going to work.'

'Dad, what time does the sun set?' Lauren asked her father that afternoon. Her book had said that the Twilight Star only

shone for ten minutes after the sun had
set and that the spell had to be perform-
ed then.

'About seven o'clock at the moment,'
her dad said. 'Why?'

'I just wondered,' Lauren said quickly.

At six-thirty her mum put supper out.

Lauren ate as fast as she could. 'May I leave the table, please?' she asked as soon as her plate was empty.

Her mum looked surprised. 'You know better, Lauren – not till everyone's finished,' she said.

So Lauren had to wait. Through the kitchen window she watched the sun dropping lower and lower in the sky. She was going to miss the sunset!

At long last her dad put his knife and fork down. 'That was delicious,' he said.

Before he had even finished speaking, Lauren had jumped to her feet. 'Can I go and see Twilight now, Mum?' she begged.

'All right,' Mrs Foster said. 'Go on.'

Lauren grabbed her jacket and ran out of the door. The book was still in the tack room. She fetched it and raced down to the paddock. Her heart was pounding in her chest. What would happen? Would the spell really work?

Twilight was standing by the gate. He whinnied when he saw her. Lauren led him towards the far corner of the field. It was shaded by trees and hidden from the house by the stable block.

As soon as they were out of sight of the house, Lauren carefully pulled a single hair out of Twilight's mane, opened the book and took the flower out of her pocket. The gold spots on the petals seemed to glow in the last rays of the sun.

She looked up. The final curve of the sun was just sinking on the horizon. Lauren's eyes narrowed as she searched for the star. But there was nothing. Maybe she had missed it? Twilight whickered.

'Ssh, Twilight,' Lauren said. She turned and patted his neck. Then she looked back up into the sky, and she gasped. High above her, a star had appeared. It was time for the spell!

'Please work,' Lauren whispered. She took a deep, trembling breath and began to tear the petals off the flower. As she did so, she read the spell out.

*Twilight Star, Twilight Star,*
*Twinkling high above so far.*
*Shining light, shining bright,*
*Will you grant my wish tonight?*
*Let my little horse forlorn*
*Be at last a unicorn!*

As she read the last word, she held her breath.

Nothing happened.

Lauren looked down at the petals in her hand and felt a wave of disappointment hit her. It was just a story after all.

She looked at Twilight and felt tears prickle in her eyes. She had so badly wanted him to be a unicorn.

Swallowing hard, she dropped the

petals on the ground.

There was a flash of purple light, so bright that it made Lauren shut her eyes. When she opened them again, she gasped.

Twilight had disappeared!

# CHAPTER
# Nine

Lauren swung around, looking for
Twilight. A snow-white unicorn was
flying in the sky behind her. Its hooves
and horn gleamed silver and its mane and
tail swirled around it.

'Twilight?' Lauren gasped.

'Yes,' the unicorn said. 'It's me. It feels a
bit wobbly up here. This is the first time
I've flown. Whoops . . .' He flew down

through the air towards Lauren, narrowly missing a low branch. With a kick of his hind legs, he landed on the grass beside her. 'Hello,' he said, walking over and nuzzling her.

Although Twilight's words rang out clearly in Lauren's head, his mouth didn't move.

'You can talk!' Lauren said in astonishment.

'Only while I'm in my magical shape,' Twilight told her. 'And you'll only be able to hear me if you're touching me or holding a hair from my mane.'

'I can't believe you're really a unicorn!' Lauren exclaimed.

Twilight laughed. 'Well, I am. I was

trapped in my pony body, but you freed me, Lauren, and that means you are my Unicorn Friend.'

'Unicorn Friend?' Lauren echoed.

Twilight nodded his beautiful head. 'Yes. Every unicorn is looking for a Unicorn Friend to do good deeds with.'

'So everything in that book is true?' Lauren gasped.

'Everything,' Twilight replied, merrily tossing his mane. He knelt down by bending his forelegs. 'Climb on my back and let's try flying together. You'll have to excuse me if I'm a bit wobbly.'

Lauren took hold of his mane and mounted. 'What if I fall off?'

'You can't fall while I am in my

magical shape,' Twilight said. 'Unicorn
magic will keep you safe.'

Lauren grabbed his mane and he
plunged forward into a canter.

'Whoa . . . hold on tight!' Twilight
called.

Twilight's hooves skimmed across the
grass and the ground dropped away. 'Here
we go!' he called to her.

His back legs kicked down powerfully
and with a jolt they flew up into the air,
lurching from side to side.

'Don't worry, I'll soon get the hang of
this,' Twilight said confidently.

Lauren held on tight. 'Wow!' she gasped
as she looked down.

Twilight surged upwards towards the

stars and the wind streamed through
Lauren's hair as they settled into a steadier
pace. 'This is amazing!' she cried.

She looked down. Below her she could
see her house and the woods.

Suddenly Lauren caught sight of a
figure walking out of the trees. A white
terrier dog with a black patch trotted at
the person's side. 'It's Mrs Fontana!' she
exclaimed.

The old lady looked up and raised her
hand in greeting. 'Hello there!' she called.

Twilight swooped towards her and
landed lightly on the soft grass.

Lauren scrambled off Twilight's back.
'Mrs Fontana!' she gasped.

Mrs Fontana smiled at Lauren. 'I see

## ✳ *My Secret Unicorn* ✳

you've found yourself a friend.'

Lauren nodded. 'Thank you for giving me the book!' she said.

'It was time it had a new owner,' Mrs Fontana replied. 'But you must promise to guard the secret carefully. A unicorn's powers can attract bad people who want to use the magic selfishly. You must not

tell a soul. Do you understand?'

At first Lauren felt disappointed. She had been thinking how amazed her mum and dad would be when she told them. But she could see the sense in what Mrs Fontana was saying. 'I understand,' she said. 'And I promise I won't tell anyone.'

'Good,' Mrs Fontana said. 'Now,' she went on, seeming to produce a piece of paper out of thin air. 'I will give you the Undoing Spell that will turn Twilight back into a pony. Say it when you return home.'

With that, Mrs Fontana handed the paper to Lauren and Lauren read the words:

*Twilight Star, Twilight Star,*
*Twinkling high above so far,*
*Protect this secret from prying eyes*
*And return my unicorn to his disguise.*
*His magical shape is for my eyes only,*
*Let him be once more a pony.*

'Keep Twilight's secret, Lauren,' Mrs
Fontana reminded her.

'I will,' Lauren promised.

Twilight bent his knees again and
Lauren climbed on to his back. With two
bounds he cantered across the grass and
rose up into the sky.

'Bye, Mrs Fontana!' Lauren called,
catching hold of his mane.

The old lady raised her hand. 'Use the

magic well, my dear,' she called and, with
that, she and Walter disappeared into the
dark wood.

Twilight and Lauren flew through the
sky. Lauren thought she had never felt
happier or more excited. There was so
much to see. They flew over the woods
and rivers, and Mrs Fontana's bookshop,
and finally they flew out over the
mountains that rose behind Granger's
Farm.

At last they returned to the paddock. As
they flew down, Lauren suddenly
remembered about her parents.

'Twilight!' she gasped. 'I hope Mum
and Dad aren't worried about me.'

'Don't worry,' Twilight told her. 'We haven't been gone very long.'

'Oh, Twilight,' Lauren said, 'this is all so exciting!'

Twilight nodded eagerly. 'And the excitement's only just beginning. Soon we'll be having all sorts of adventures together.' He nuzzled her leg. 'Oh, Lauren. I'm so happy you're my Unicorn Friend.'

Lauren hugged him. 'And I'm so happy you're my unicorn.'

As Lauren dismounted, she took the piece of paper that Mrs Fontana had given her out of her pocket. Slowly she read out the Undoing Spell. As she spoke the last word, there was a flash of

blinding purple light and suddenly
Lauren felt cold air on her face. She
opened her eyes. She was still standing
beside Twilight, but he was no longer a
unicorn; he was just a small grey pony.
For a moment Lauren wondered if she'd

imagined everything, but then she looked down at the piece of paper in her hand. No, it had been real.

Twilight snuffled at her hair and she felt a surge of excitement fizz inside her.

'Goodnight,' Lauren whispered, kissing him in delight. Then, picking up the book from the grass, she turned and ran to the house.

As she hurried in, Buddy bounded over to greet her, almost knocking her down in his excitement.

Her dad was washing up the supper dishes at the sink and her mum was pouring Max a drink.

'How was Twilight?' her mum asked.

'He was fine,' Lauren said. 'I . . . I think

I might just go up to my room and read for a while.'

She went upstairs and sat down by her bedroom window. Twilight was grazing in his paddock. Seeming to sense that Lauren was looking at him, he raised his head and whinnied.

A broad grin crept across Lauren's face.

Her new pony had turned out to be her secret unicorn.

What adventures they were going to have!

# My Secret Unicorn

When Lauren recites a secret spell, her pony
Twilight turns into a beautiful unicorn with magical
powers! Together Lauren and Twilight learn how to
use their magic to help their friends.

**The Magic Spell**
Linda Chapman

**Dreams Come True**
Linda Chapman

**Flying High**
Linda Chapman

**Starlight Surprise**
Linda Chapman

**Stronger Than Magic**
Linda Chapman

Look out for more *My Secret Unicorn* adventures

# My Secret Unicorn

Lauren's nervous about starting a new school and making new friends. Can Twilight's magical powers help?

Look out for more **My Secret Unicorn** adventures

# My Secret Unicorn

Lauren's friend Jessica is finding life at home difficult. Lauren and Twilight want to help her but can they persuade her to trust them?

Look out for more *My Secret Unicorn* adventures

# my Secret Unicorn

There are rumours going round school that there is a haunted treehouse by the creek. It's up to Lauren and Twilight to solve the spooky mystery!

Look out for more *my Secret Unicorn* adventures

# My Secret Unicorn

On one of their evening fly-arounds Twilight starts
to feel ill and he and Lauren have to stop exploring
and return home. Can they find something stronger
than magic to help Twilight get bettter. . .?

Look out for more **My Secret Unicorn** adventures